# Nuptse and Lhotse in Nepal

Jocey Asnong

Spelling, village names, mountain heights, and other information about Nepal often change between different maps and books.

Nuptse and Lhotse in Nepal/ Written and Illustrated by Jocey Asnong

ISBN 978-1-897530-04-7

Asnong, Jocelyn, 1973-
Nuptse and Lhotse in Nepal / written and illustrated by Jocey Asnong.

ISBN 978-1-897530-04-7

1. Nepal--Juvenile fiction.  2. Himalaya Mountains--Juvenile fiction.
I. Title.
PS8601.S592N86 2008        jC813'.6              C2008-906012-1

**Mixed Sources**
Cert no. SW-COC-001271
© 1996 FSC

Published by 4th Floor Press, Inc.
www.4thfloorpress.com
1st Printing 2008
Printed in Canada

www.cautiousleroy.com

# Dedicated
## To
Aven Morgan
**May you one day go to the high-up snowy places.**

# Once upon a time,
## a while ago,
### maybe sometime last year...

NuptSe

...there lived two extraordinarily

Things about Nuptse (Nup-see):

a little sister cat,
an artist,
a daydreamer,
and a scaredy cat.

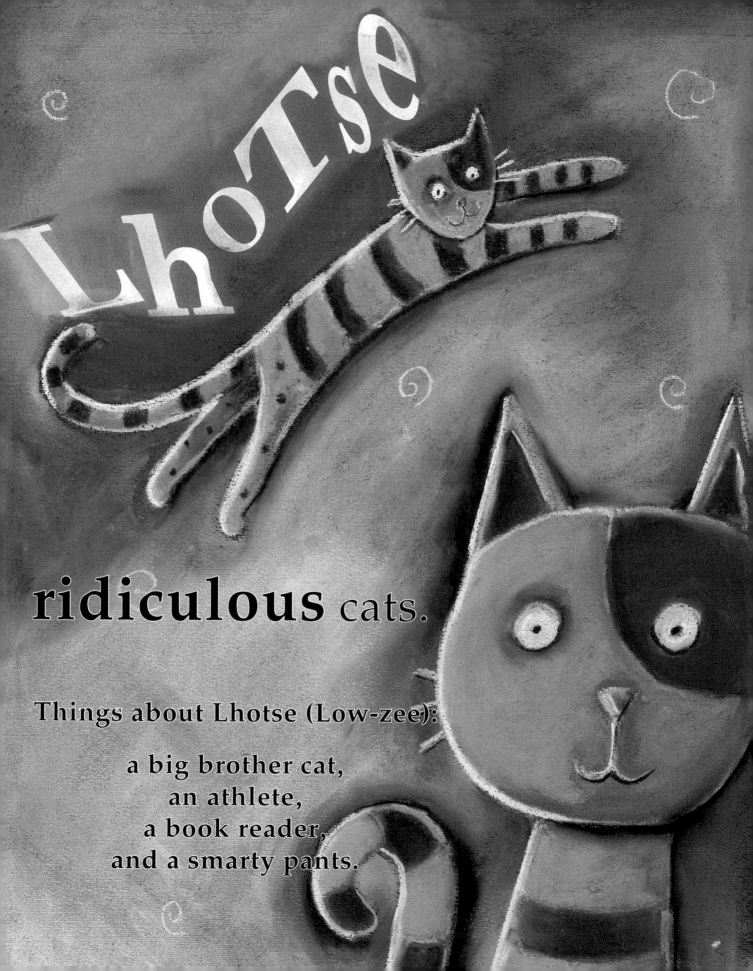

LhoTse

ridiculous cats.

Things about Lhotse (Low-zee):

a big brother cat,
an athlete,
a book reader,
and a smarty pants.

**Anyways,** a few minutes past the time that it was at that particular moment, Nuptse and Lhotse were behind the upside down clock looking for Nuptse's lost marbles.

"Look what I found!" said Lhotse. "It's an old map of a place called Mount Everest." He leaned over the dusty map. Nuptse began pointing excitedly at some words on the map, and then she immediately sneezed six times.

"Our NAMES are on here!" she exclaimed. "There's a Mount Nuptse and a Mount Lhotse right beside Mount Everest!"

"It looks like our mountains are in between these two lands, Nepal and Tibet," said Lhotse.

"Oh, Lhotse, we absolutely HAVE to go see our mountains right away!" said Nuptse.

"What is it?" asked Nuptse.

TIBET

Mount Nuptse

Mount Everest

Mount Lhotse

"Our Names are on this map!" squealed Lhotse.

KATHMANDU

NEPAL

So, faster than you can say Mount Everest backwards, they packed their things and chased each other outside to Lhotse's purring airplane.

"Did you know that Mount Everest is the tallest mountain in the world?" yelled Lhotse as they flew through the clouds. "Our mountains hug Mount Everest on each side. Isn't that fascinating, Nuptse? Nuptse! Are you even listening to me? What are you doing back there?"

"I wonder what colours our mountains will be," said Nuptse dreamily. "Mine will be purple, or red, no, definitely purple, I think. Or baby blue, my favourite colour! Oh, I do hope my Mount Nuptse is baby blue!"

**37** seconds to fly to Nepal," said Lhotse.

*tuk tuks*

*stupa*

Quietly, Nuptse sang to herself,
"Cat-man-doo, cat-man-doo, we
like you, cat-man-doo," as she
followed Lhotse out of the city and
into the hills.

*monkey*

*holy cow*

*temples*

Definition
of
a
"Trek"

To walk a
long long
long long
long long
long long
long long
long time
for many
many many
many many
many many
many many
many many
many many
many many
days on
very very
very ve
very ve
very ve
very ve
very ve
sore feet

The two cats walked up and down

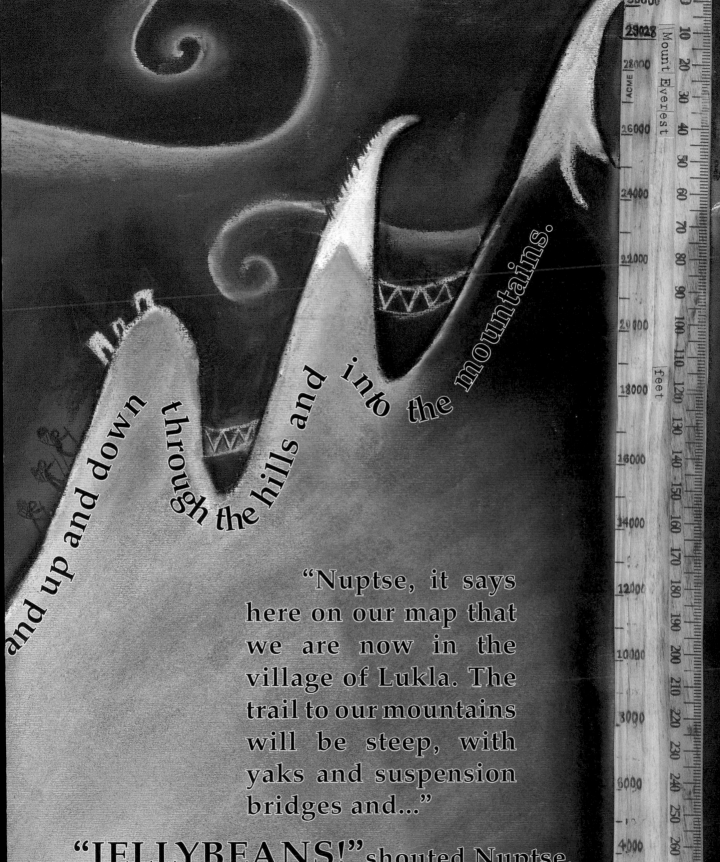

and up and down
through the hills and
into the mountains.

"Nuptse, it says
here on our map that
we are now in the
village of Lukla. The
trail to our mountains
will be steep, with
yaks and suspension
bridges and..."

"JELLYBEANS!" shouted Nuptse.

Mount Everest
29028
ACME
feet

30000
28000
26000
24000
22000
20000
18000
16000
14000
12000
10000
8000
6000
4000
2000

"Jellybeans? What are you talking about, Nuptse? You can't just say that the trail is full of jellybeans. It doesn't make any sense."

"Then how do you explain this?" Nuptse popped a green jellybean into her mouth and grinned. She had the funny look she got when she was keeping a secret.

"Where did you find that?" asked Lhotse. He looked at her curiously. "Wait, what's in your backpack, Nuptse?"

"Um, just some stuff for climbing mountains." Nuptse shrugged.

"Your pack is FULL of jellybeans, Nuptse!"

"I know. It's... it's all I brought," said Nuptse. "I eat them every time I feel scared."

# ·What should be in a backpack·

WARM jacket

WARM Hat

mittens

underwears

first aid

water & filter

socks

Long johns

sleeping bag

toothbrush stuff

# ·What absolutely should never be in a backpack·

catnip mice

T.V.

grand piano

dress-up boots

angry bees

heavy weights

"Can we stay here tonight? It's starting to get dark," said Nuptse as they walked towards a group of colourful houses. "Only if this is the village of Namche Bazaar," answered Lhotse. He checked the map again. "Nam-chee-BIZARRE? What kind of name is that?"

"Nuptse! This is the land of the Sherpa people. They have lived here for hundreds of years and are famous for climbing mountains. We need to be on our best behaviour here."

MOON Light LOUNGe

"Can best behaviour include dressing up like a Sherpa and making up songs about Mount Nuptse all night?"

The Sun was just saying good morning to the sleepy Moon when the cats woke up the next day.

"Guess what, Nuptse? We are **higher** than anywhere we have **ever** been, and we still have to go **farther** up and then **up again**. To help us breathe, we need to take lots of catnaps so our hearts and lungs can get **stronger** in the thin air."

"What does mountain sickness feel like?" asked Nuptse.

"You get giggly, dizzy, tummy achy, and forgetful," answered Lhotse.

"And would it also make me want to walk around in circles until I fall down?"

"Yes, but Nuptse, you feel like doing that every day! You do not have **mountain sickness**."

Symptoms of Mountain Sickness....the giggles....dizzy...sleepy... tummy Ache....forgetfulness....WALKING on

A little while later, some time the next day, the cats had to cross a high wobbly wooden bridge over the Dudh Khosi River.

"That river looks hungry," whimpered Nuptse as she looked over the railing.

"Just follow me, like this." Lhotse skipped across the bridge to the other side. Nuptse carefully tiptoed across after him, but the bridge began to swing and swoop and creak and groan.

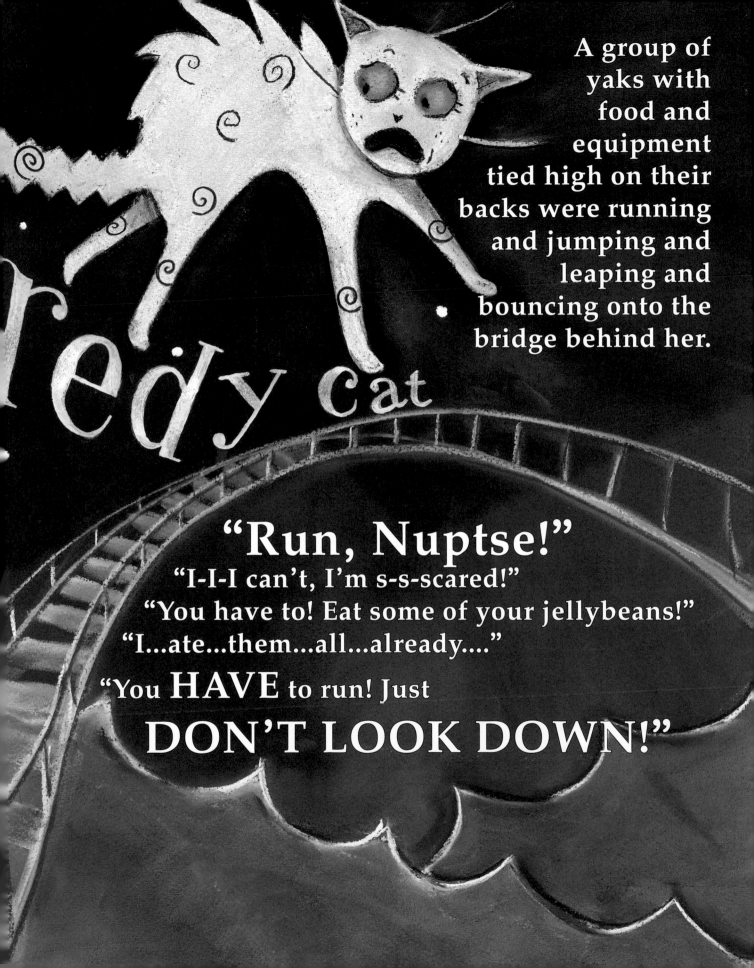

"**Wait!** Stop telling the story for a minute," interrupted Lhotse. "Do you really want to have the yaks in our book, Nuptse? It might be too scary to read."

"We have to put this part in to show how brave I was and stopped being scared," Nuptse said.

"But you're still scared of water, the dark, strawberry jam, and your own shadow!" Lhotse laughed.

"But not yaks anymore! Now, LET'S KEEP TELLING OUR STORY."

Nuptse took a deep breath, looked at Lhotse standing safely on the other side of the bridge, and began to run. The yaks came running right behind her.

"I DID IT! I DID IT! Did you see how fast I ran, Lhotse?"

"It was amazing! I've never seen you run so fast. I don't know if I've ever even seen you run!" said Lhotse, hugging her.

"We should let you rest at the next place on our map. It's called the Tengboche Monastery."

eight lives, nine lives, one life, two lives three

lives, five lives, six lives, seven lives

One life, two lives, three lives, four

3

5

7

9

4

6

2

8

"Tang-bo-shay, tang-bo-shay,"

OM MANi PADME HUM OM HUM OM

Nuptse sang as she followed Lhotse up the hill and into the painted monastery. A room full of monks were praying.

"Nuptse, we wish you peace and bravery," the monks chanted quietly.

"Did they just say my name?" she whispered.

"I think they said 'Namaste.' It's a way to say hello."

"Lhotse, we wish you joy and happiness," chanted the monks again.

"Did you hear that, Lhotse? I am sure they are talking about us. How do they know who we are?"

"Ssshhh," whispered a monk. He placed a white silk scarf around Nuptse's neck and another one around Lhotse's neck. "Be on your way. You are almost at your mountains."

The cats had made it to a place called Base Camp. With frostbitten whiskers, they looked out from their tent through millions of falling snowflakes.

"We need to find the Khumbu Icefall," said Lhotse, checking their map. Nuptse wandered a few feet away from him.

"Does the Khumbu look like a huge frozen waterfall covered in snow?" she asked.

"Yes! Can you see it?"

"It's over here, right under the big fat toes of our mountains," shouted Nuptse through the snowstorm.
"Nuptse, where are you? Where did you go?"

"I'm over here. I want to climb my mountain. There's a ladder and ropes!" Nuptse said, her voice trailing off. "Let me just check the map first, Nuptse. Nuptse? NUPTSE!"

"It's just like walking in ice cream," yelled Nuptse. "Vanilla tuna fish sundae! Butterscotch salmon sorbet! Peppermint catnip popsicles!"

She ran up the snowy slopes, following the ropes and ladders she had found.

"Nuptse! Nuptse, wait for me! You're going the wrong way," yelled Lhotse after her.

The wind whistled his words away. He could just see the end of Nuptse's tail disappearing into the blizzard.

**Definition of a blizzard:**
To get very very very very very very very lost in a cold cold cold cold cold cold cold cold place with millions and millions and millions and millions of snowflakes.

"Lhotse, we are almost at the top!" She stopped to look around her.

"Lhotse? Where are you?" It was very quiet. Snowflakes swirled around her.

"Lhotse?" Nuptse's heart beat loudly.

"Lho-tse....?" Nuptse hiccupped.

"NUPTSE?
Is that
you up there?"
called Lhotse
out into the storm.

"LHOTSE!" Nuptse gasped. "Oh, I am so
glad to see you!"
"Nuptse, I was so scared. I couldn't find you in
the snowstorm and I thought I lost you forever!"
said Lhotse.
"Look, we are almost at the top of
**my mountain!"**

"Nuptse, do
you realize
that we have
just about
climbed . . .

# MOUNT

## the tallest mountain

"Don't worry, Nuptse. I know

# EVEREST

## in the world!

"Oh no! I thought I was climbing Mount Nuptse," sniffled Nuptse. She sat in the snow and wiped a tear away with her mitten. "We've come so far, Lhotse. Will we ever get to see the mountains we were named after?"

## exactly what we can do."

Nuptse and Lhotse

stepped together onto Mount Everest.

"I can see the top of Mount Nuptse and Mount Lhotse from here!" said Nuptse. She danced in a tiny circle on the top of the mountain and clapped her mittens together.

"Lhotse, there are hundreds of mountains here! I want to stay here forever!"

"Look, Nuptse!" Lhotse pointed. "Don't you think our mountains kind of look like us?" Nuptse and Lhotse looked at each other and giggled.

"We did it! Do you think anyone will ever believe us?" asked Nuptse.

"I know! We'll leave our scarves and a picture of us! Then everyone who comes all the way up here will know that we did it!"

# The End (almost)

"Lhotse? How do we get down from here?"

"We need to climb down."

"Climb down? Cats do NOT climb DOWN anything. I do NOT climb DOWN anything. I am NOT climbing down Mount Everest!"

"Nuptse, how do you think everyone else gets off of here?"

"I can't even think about it. Maybe I'll just stay up here."

"You can't stay up here, Nuptse. What if I told you that a Sherpa is coming to help us climb down?"

"Really? How did he know we would need help?" asked Nuptse excitedly.

"He followed us to make sure we would be safe. We'll go slowly and carefully and we'll all make it back to our homes so we can have more adventures!"

"I'll think about it. Let me just say goodbye to my mountain first."

# "Finally, The End"

# Lhotse's Interesting Facts

- Mount Lhotse is about 8516 m (27890 feet) high and it is the 4th highest mountain in the world.

- Mount Lhotse is taller than Mount Nuptse.

- The name for Mount Everest in Nepal is Sagarmatha. It is 8848 m (29029 feet) high and gets taller every year.

- One of the best times to CLIMB Mount Everest is in May before the monsoon rain.

- Many climbers from all over the world try each year to climb Mount Everest.

- Mount Everest can be climbed from Nepal starting near the Khumbu Icefall.

- It takes most people several weeks of training on the mountain to get to the very top of Mount Everest and get back to Base Camp.

- Sir Edmund Hillary from New Zealand and Tenzing Norgay from Nepal were the first to climb Mount Everest at 11:30 am on May 29, 1953.

- In Nepal, a porter is a person who carries heavy baskets of supplies for villages or bags and backpacks for the trekkers.

- A Yak (or Nak for females) is a mammal that looks like a big, hairy cow. They carry supplies on their backs, provide milk, butter, and cheese, and their hair can be used for wool.

- Lhotse's favourite food in Nepal was Daal Baht (rice, lentil soup, and special spices). Delicious!

# Nuptse's Exciting Facts

- Mount Nuptse is about 7879 m (27755 feet) high, and is either the 19th, 20th, or 21st highest mountain in the world depending on which list you check.

- Mount Nuptse is shorter but prettier and pointier than Mount Lhotse.

- The name for Mount Everest in Tibet is Chomolungma. There is hardly any air at the top to breathe.

- One of the other best times to SEE Mount Everest is in October or November after the monsoon rain.

- Many people from all over the world come to Nepal each year just to see the highest mountains.

- Mount Everest can also be climbed from Tibet starting near the Rongbuk Glacier.

- It takes most people about 15 -18 days of trekking along dirt trails to get to see Mount Everest and get back to Kathmandu.

- George Mallory and Andrew Irvine tried to be the first to climb Mount Everest on June 8, 1924. It is a mystery whether they made it all the way to the top before they disappeared.

- In Nepal, a monk (bhikkhus) or nun (bhikkhunis) are people who have taken vows to study Buddhist wisdom and meditations. They may live in a monastery.

- A Yeti is a legend about a wandering snowman that looks like a big, hairy person. No one knows for sure if it is the truth or make-believe.

- Nuptse's favourite food in Nepal was momos (spicy dumplings) and fingerchips (fried potatoes). Yum!

Jocey Asnong was raised by a pack of wild pencil crayons in a house made of paper and stories in a land full of maple trees. After many years of Illustration school, she moved to the mountains of Alberta, Canada, so that she could wear mittens most of the year. When she is not shivering in a Mount Everest blizzard, she chases her cats around her home studio and works as a freelance artist. She has travelled 2 times, 4 months, and seven days in Nepal and can't wait to return.

www.cautiousleroy.com

Five percent of the profits from this book will be donated to organizations that protect Nepal and the people who live there.

**SERVE Nepal (SA Foundation):** dedicated to fighting and preventing exploitation and trafficking in Nepal. One person, one family, and one community at a time.
*www.serve-nepal.org*

**Kathmandu Environmental Education Program (KEEP):** provides information to travellers and ensures the future ecological and cultural prosperity of Nepal through positive impact tourism and outreach project work.
*www.keepnepal.org*

**International Porter Protection Group (IPPG):** improves the conditions of mountain porters in the tourism industry worldwide.
*www.ippg.net*

## Most of this story is true, except for the parts that are not...

In the summer of 2003, one extraordinary sleepless night would completely change the direction of my life. By 4 am, I had made the decision that I would go to Nepal in two months' time. The moment I arrived in the Khumbu-Mount Everest region, I knew that I was in way over my head, that I was physically unprepared, and that I was definitely going to have to face some of my biggest fears. It was also extremely possible that despite how scared I was, I was already falling hopelessly in love with Nepal. As I walked through the Himalayas those next two months, this story began to breathe within me. This story was a part of the landscape, in the songs danced around the tea house stove each night, and in the faces of the people in each village. Returning to my home in Canada, I began longing for this country that had become such a part of me. I started illustrating and writing this story as a way to remember and to give back in some small way all that was given to me.

To the people of Nepal, Dhanyabhad (thank you).

# A  Mountain of thank yous
## also

In Nepal
To those of you who were brave enough and patient enough to share the
trails with me over the years:
To Kiley T, for agreeing to go that first time, and getting me through my
scaredy-cat moments.
To Dave C, for sharing your fingerchips and friendship.
To Dominik Z, for EBC and trekker watching.
To Neil and Joyce H, for sharing bus rides, festivals, and momos, as well as
all of your continued support.
And to Arjun, Buddhi, Nawang, Sushil, and Ram, who all helped along
the way.

At Home
To all of you who have encouraged, inspired, edited, contributed, and
believed in this story.
To my family, for filling my life with a love for stories and mountains.
To Brigid B and Nicole N, for your first draft thoughts that winter day.
To Anne B for your incredible support, and to Ray J, and Wendy L, and
everyone else at 4th Floor Press for putting all the pieces together.
To the Banff Centre Writing with Style class of 2006, for helping Nuptse
find her voice.

And Always
To J